Yellow Eyes in the Dark

CAMP
WANNA BANANA
MYSTERIES

YELLOW EYES IN THE DARK

Becky Freeman

WATERBROOK
PRESS

Yellow Eyes in the Dark
Published by WaterBrook Press
12265 Oracle Boulevard, Suite 200
Colorado Springs, Colorado 80921

ISBN 978-1-57856-351-7

Published in association with the literary agency of Alive Communications, Inc.,
7680 Goddard Street, Suite 200, Colorado Springs, CO 80920.

Published in the United States by WaterBrook Multnomah, an imprint of the Crown
Publishing Group, a division of Random House Inc., New York.

WaterBrook and its deer colophon are registered trademarks of Random House Inc.

Library of Congress Cataloging-in-Publication Data
Freeman, Becky, 1959-
    Yellow eyes in the dark / Becky Freeman.—1st ed.
        p. cm. — (Camp Wanna Banana mysteries ; 3)
        Summary: Maria and Marco search Camp Wanna Banana for Joy's missing pet spider
monkey Munch-Munch, but when they become lost and injured Maria must face her
doubts about whether God cares for her.
        ISBN 1-57856-351-8
        [1. Spider monkeys—Fiction. 2. Monkeys—Fiction. 3. Lost and found posses-
sions—Fiction. 4. Pets—Fiction. 5. Camps—Fiction. 6. Christian life. 7. Mystery and
detective stories.] I. Title.

PZ7.F874635 Ye 2001
[Fic]—dc21
                                                                    2001046799

Printed in the United States of America

To Chelsea and Hannah

Thank you, girls,
for helping your Aunt Becky out
by reading this book and making great suggestions!

CONTENTS

ACKNOWLEDGMENTS

Thank you to Erin Healy, Laura Barker, Greg Johnson, Sheila Walsh, and the Children of Faith folks for helping to make this dream of writing children's books come true!

1

MONKEY HERE, MONKEY THERE, MONKEY...NOWHERE!

Maria Garcia flipped her long black hair behind her back, shaded her eyes from the late afternoon sun with her hand, and looked up into trees ablaze with autumn color. Then she glanced over to the maze of monkey bars.

"Look at her go!" Maria said, pointing toward a small spider monkey swinging from bar to bar like a happy kid on a flying trapeze. The tiny monkey wore a bright yellow T-shirt, and a yellow bow with red polka dots was perched in the tuft of hair on top of her head.

Maria's best friend and owner of the pet monkey, Joy, nodded her ponytail full of blond curls and smiled. "Munch-Munch loves this place!"

"So do I," added Maria. She surveyed the playground equipment around her: a banana-shaped teeter-totter, a huge banana-shaped tree slide, a snack stand with a banana-shaped countertop. "Banana Bash Zone is just about everyone's favorite spot at Camp Wanna Banana."

"I know," agreed Joy, reaching to catch Munch-Munch as the screeching monkey jumped into her waiting arms. "And we're the only kids lucky enough to play here all year long, even when camp isn't in session."

"That's the best part about our dads working here," Maria agreed. Maria's papa took care of the camp's riding arena and horse stalls at Monkey Ranch. Señor Garcia groomed and cared for the horses and took kids on trail rides during camp season. He worked for Joy's father, Mr. Bigsley, who owned and ran Camp Wanna Banana.

Maria smiled and reached out for Munch-Munch, who went to her cheerfully. The small monkey wrapped her skinny, hairy arms around Maria's neck and squeezed. Maria planted a kiss on the small monkey's head. "She's soooo cute! Oh, Joy, I really, really want a pet of my own. I want something to snuggle and care for and love the way you love Munchy."

"Why don't you ask your mom for one?" Joy asked.

Maria frowned. The red and gold leaves that had been falling off the trees for the past few weeks formed piles all over the Banana Bash Zone. She kicked at them as she walked over to a banana-shaped bench with Munch-Munch and sat down. "Joy, you know my mama. She keeps the house perfectly clean and insists that it stay that way. She says dogs and cats leave hair everywhere. She doesn't even want to have a little bird or gerbil in the house because she thinks they smell and have messy cages!"

Joy sat next to Maria and put her arm around her friend. "You've got a great mom. You know how proud she is of you and Marco. And nobody cooks like she does! Her tamales and chicken enchiladas make my mouth water. But I'll admit she sure does like to keep things sparkly clean."

Whenever Joy's twin brother, Jake, and Maria's twin brother, Marco, came within yards of the Garcia front porch, Maria's mother would begin hollering, half in Spanish, half in English, out the kitchen window. *"Chicos!* Take off your muddy boots before you step a foot *en mi casa!"* ("Boys! Take off your muddy boots before you step a foot in my house!") Sometimes Maria was embarrassed by her mother's tidiness. Sometimes it felt like Mama cared more about having a perfect house than anything else!

The Bigsley household, on the other hand, seemed to be more interested in fun. *In fact,* Maria thought with a smile, *Jake and Joy's home seems like a circus sometimes.* Mrs. Bigsley was always singing some silly song or laughing out loud with the kids at Munch-Munch's latest antics. She nicknamed Jake, Joy, Maria, and Marco "the Twiblings"—a combination of "twins" and "siblings"—just for fun. Jake was usually running around in some crazy clownish getup—like oversize rubber boots or a pail hat. Joy acted much like a ringmaster, trying to gain some control and order of the chaos usually brewing around her.

"I wish my family were more like yours," Maria said wistfully as Munch-Munch jumped down from the bench to play in a pile of leaves. "I especially wish my mother were more fun, like your mom."

"What?" Joy asked in surprise. "My mother can never find anything she's looking for—she'll never get organized! If I didn't wash my own clothes, I'd have to wear my bathrobe to school. *Your* mom always washes your clothes and has them neatly folded and ready to hang up in your room. Our house is never as clean and orderly as yours. Your home is so peaceful and quiet—"

"And boring," added Maria, faking a long yawn.

Munch-Munch jumped out of the leaves with a happy screech and dashed toward the junglegym.

Joy laughed. "It's funny how we always seems to think other kids have a better deal."

"Yeah," agreed Maria. "I guess no family is perfect. I love my mama, you know. I just wish she'd lighten up a little."

"And I wish my mom would clean up a little," Joy replied with a grin.

Maria smiled. Joy was one of the few people Maria could just be herself with. She never worried about what Joy might think of her, because Joy always seemed to think the best, no matter what. Maria pulled her legs up on the bench and rested her chin on her knees.

"Do you think God would answer my prayer if I prayed for a pet?" Maria asked quietly. "Could He maybe change Mama's mind?"

Joy took a minute to answer. "Well, the Bible says God cares even when a tiny sparrow falls to the ground," Joy said thoughtfully. "And if He cares about little birds that fall out of their nests, then I'm sure He cares about you wanting a pet of your own. Let's start praying about it and see what happens, okay?"

"That would be great," Maria agreed. "What if we—"

She was cut off by the sharp sound of snapping twigs and a wild rustling of leaves. A large swirl of gray fur leaped from behind one tree to another at the edge of the Banana Bash Zone and disappeared as quickly as it had come into view.

"What was *that?*" Joy asked, her eyes wide.

Maria turned to grab Munch-Munch. But the monkey was nowhere to be seen.

"Where's Munchy?"

"I don't know," Joy answered, worry in her voice. "She was right here a minute ago! She never runs off unless—"

"She's playing hide-and-seek," Maria finished,

knowing how the little pet liked to play games. The girls were up now, starting to search.

"Or unless she sees something that makes her really curious," Joy said.

"You don't think she went after that...that... whatever that furry gray thing was?"

Joy's eyes grew wide. "What if that thing went after *her?* We'd better start looking for her—and quick! *Munnn-chyyyyyy!*"

"Come here, girl!" Maria joined in. The two girls hurried around the Bash Zone and the edge of the nearby woods, looking everywhere the missing monkey could have hidden. But after a long time of searching and running and calling her name, they still couldn't find Munch-Munch.

Breathless, Maria said, "We've got to go get Jake and Marco to help us search!"

Joy, who was usually the one in control, suddenly looked small and helpless. A tear fell down her cheek. Maria could hardly bear to see Joy so upset. Acting more sure than she felt, Maria hugged her friend and said, "Don't worry, Joy. We'll find her. Like you said, God even cares about sparrows. I'm sure He cares for a lost spider monkey, too. And the girls who love her."

2

STARING YELLOW EYES

arco!" Maria yelled. "Jake! You've got to help us!"

Joy and Maria ran down the trail to Monkey Ranch, where their brothers were grooming two of the horses. Maria's lungs stung with the sharp dryness of the cool Arizona mountain air. Jake and Marco stood back to back between Brick, Jake's favorite chestnut mare, and the new black stallion named Lightning. Jake brushed Brick's back while Marco bent over Lightning's shoe, trying to dislodge a rock.

A local couple had donated Lightning to the camp two weeks earlier before moving to a smaller home near Phoenix. Lightning was a little skittish in his new surroundings, and Maria's papa had been working with the horse every day to help settle him.

"What's up?" asked Marco, who bolted upright at the very moment Jake turned toward the girls' voices. Marco's head met Jake's elbow with a loud crack, and both boys fell wincing onto the hay-covered stable floor.

"Are you sure we need them for this?" Joy asked Maria.

Maria rolled her eyes helplessly.

Jake stood again, grasping his funny bone. Pieces of hay were stuck in his spiky blond hair, making it look even more like a haystack than it usually did.

Marco stayed on the floor rubbing his head. "At your service, ladies," he managed with a half smile. "The Dos Amigos Detectives: Ever Brave and Ready to Save."

I don't know if they are Brave and Ready or Dumb and Dumber, thought Maria. *But either way, we really could use their help.*

"We can't find Munchy," Joy started in a rush.

"She was playing with us in the Banana Bash Zone, and then she disappeared."

"Did you look for any clues?" Jake asked.

"What kind of clues?" Maria asked.

"Anything that would tell you where she wandered," Marco explained, getting to his feet. "Any evidence that someone—or something—might have taken her."

Maria looked at Joy, then back at the boys. "There was this gray blur—it was probably some kind of animal—that rushed by us right before she disappeared. We're thinking maybe Munchy was curious enough to run after it. You know how she's always chasing dogs and cats."

"What size and shape was the gray blur?" asked Marco, reaching into his back pocket for a pad and pencil. Maria shook her head slowly and with annoyance. Marco—Mr. Scientific—loved nothing more than to investigate details. Like how many steps it took to get from their house to the boat dock and back. Or the names of every tree on Camp Wanna Banana property. Or five ways to stop a wound from bleeding. He collected facts the way Maria collected toy animals.

"I really think we should start looking before it gets dark," she said, ignoring his question. No one seemed to hear her.

"It happened so fast," Joy explained to Marco. "But I think it was bigger than a dog. And smaller than a horse."

"It had four legs, I'm pretty sure," Maria said, trying to be helpful.

Marco sighed. "Well, duh, Maria. Most animals *do* have four legs, don't they?"

Jake shook his head and picked up the currycombs and brushes to put them away. "Girls, girls," he said, walking toward the wall where the grooming tools were hung. "Real detectives have to be more alert. You've got to pay attention to details!" With that, Jake accidentally stepped in a bucket of oats. He quickly stepped back out, trying to pretend nothing had happened. If Maria had not been so worried about Munch-Munch, she would have enjoyed a good laugh at this. Jake was always talking big and important as he skipped and tripped his way through life.

Maria felt a rush of goose bumps cover her arms as a late-fall breeze came through the stable. She noticed that Joy was shivering too, probably with some doubts about whether they would find her beloved pet. Reaching up, Maria pulled down two heavy fleece jackets from hooks hanging on the stable door. One belonged to Mr. Bigsley, the other to Mr. Garcia. She handed Mr. Bigsley's to her friend and put the other one on herself. It hung past her knees. Joy smiled weakly and snuggled inside the thick, fuzzy lining of her dad's favorite "stompin' around the barn" coat.

"Okay, Mr. Smart Guy Detectives," Maria said as she buttoned her papa's red plaid jacket around her. "What do you two think we should do next?"

Marco fingered the bump emerging beneath his thick, dark hair. "Well, we don't have time to walk back to the Banana Bash Zone to search for Munchy before it gets dark. Why don't we saddle up these horses and ride over there before the sun sets? It'll only take a few minutes."

"No, Marco," Maria said, worried. "Papa said he doesn't want us riding Lightning yet. He doesn't think the horse is ready."

"But look how calm he's been while I brushed him!" Marco pointed to the new horse, who indeed was standing as still as a horse on a merry-go-round. He grabbed a blanket and threw it over Lightning's back. "And it's not like he's never been ridden before. Here's what we're going to do: Jake and Joy—take Brick and go see if your mom or dad can come help us. Maria and I will ride Lightning over to the Banana Bash Zone and check for clues while we wait for you."

Maria didn't argue. Time was too short. She could see the sky outside the stable doors beginning to turn sunset pink. Still, Maria had a nagging feeling she should try to talk Marco out of taking the stallion. They should saddle up a quiet, more reliable horse, Maria thought. But Marco had already heaved the saddle onto Lightning. And the need to find Munch-Munch seemed more important than anything else. She put her worries about Lightning out of her mind and began to help Marco.

Within minutes, the foursome had mounted their horses and was trotting off on a search-and-rescue-a-monkey mission.

Maria clung to her brother's waist as they rode Lightning down the trail to the Banana Bash Zone at a quick trot. Because Lightning was faster and more eager, they were soon far ahead of Jake and Joy. In fact, as the wooded camp trail twisted and turned, Jake and Joy completely disappeared from Maria's sight.

Maria felt the weight of Marco's backpack bouncing gently against her papa's bulky jacket. Marco had suggested she wear it so she could ride behind him more comfortably. Maria couldn't help smiling a little. Marco and Jake were always on the lookout for a mystery or an adventure. They kept their backpacks filled with anything they might need in an emergency. The two boys wore them everywhere—even to the library and Sunday school. (Maria's papa once saw Marco tuck a first-aid kit into his backpack before church. "Son," he teased, "are you worried about somebody fainting and knocking themselves out while reciting Bible verses or something?")

Something drew Maria's attention to a thick grove of trees ahead of them and to the side of the trail. The leaves on a nearby bush stirred.

"Look!" Maria said, pointing. "Over there!"

Marco turned toward the source of the rustling. "Is that you, Munchy?" he asked. "Are you playing hide-and-seek, girl?"

No sound came from behind the bush, but now Maria and Marco were close enough to see two large yellow eyes staring steadily back at them.

And they were definitely not the eyes of a small, friendly monkey.

3

WILD RIDE!

The yellow-eyed animal must be afraid of us,
Maria thought, surprised that she didn't feel
scared. It sprang from behind the bush and darted
across the trail right in front of them. Maria couldn't
make out anything but a grayish white blur—just like
the one she'd seen before Munchy disappeared.

Although Maria wasn't afraid, the same could not
be said for the big black horse she and Marco rode.
The gray creature, whatever it was, scared the thunder out of Lightning.

When the mysterious animal brushed past the stallion's legs before jumping out of sight, the frightened horse whinnied and reared, nearly tossing Maria off his back. With every bit of strength she had, she clung to Marco's shirt. "Marco!" she screamed. *"Hold on!"*

"I am!" he hollered into the wind. And with that, Lightning darted off the trail and into the woods.

"Whoa, boy!" Marco commanded, pulling tight on the reins. But Lightning was too terrified to notice. His heaving, running, sweating body was determined to go instead of whoa. Dodging tree limbs and scratchy bushes, Marco and Maria hung on for the ride of their lives.

Faster and farther Lightning ran, his hoofs pounding as loud as Maria's heartbeat. *When is he going to stop? He's going to throw us! I'm about to fall off…can't hold on much longer…*

Lightning finally broke through the woods and into a clearing, leaving a trail of red, yellow, and orange leaves flying in his wake. Without trees to slow him, the frantic horse broke from a canter into a full gallop—away, away, away from Camp Wanna Banana and all that looked familiar to the Garcia twins. *Why didn't Marco listen to me?* Maria was as

17

angry as she was scared now. *We should never have taken this crazy horse out of the barn—and Marco knew it! This is all his fault!*

Neither Marco nor Maria said a word as their wild-eyed ride sped away into unfamiliar territory. It took all their concentration just to hang on to the runaway horse. The twins managed to stay in the saddle for what seemed like forever, but just as the sun began to slip behind a rugged mountain peak to the west, Lightning reared again and let out a terrified neigh.

Maria felt herself hurtling toward the ground. She watched Marco flail in midair and, out of the corner of her eye, saw the horse bolt away.

Then everything went fuzzy and cold.

For a few seconds Maria lay on her side in the dirt, unmoving, too hurt and afraid to move. Then, in the fog of her rattled mind, she remembered the oddest thing: Joy's kind voice saying, "God even cares about sparrows that fall to the ground…"

Dear Father, Maria prayed silently, desperately. *Please help us. We are two sparrows fallen to the ground. And we need You now.*

4

DOUBLE TROUBLE

aria?" Maria opened her eyes and saw her
brother standing over her in the last glow
of sunset. He was holding his left arm with his right
hand, wincing with pain. "Maria?" he said again. "Are
you all right?"

"I...uh...I think so," Maria answered, moving
her arms and legs a bit to see whether they were all
present and unhurt. "What about you?"

"I think I may have broken my arm," he said,
breathing hard. "It hurts too bad to be just a bruise."

Maria tried to roll over, but the crazy backpack was in her way. Slipping out of it awkwardly, she sat up and with relief noted that she wasn't injured. She also noticed, gratefully, that she'd landed just in front of an enormous prickly pear cactus, narrowly missing its sharp spines. *That would NOT have been fun,* she thought. She and Marco were on hard, packed, dusty ground surrounded by stubby trees and coarse undergrowth. A jagged rockface, full of nooks and crannies, rose to the sky a short distance in front of them.

Maria started to stand up, but waves of pain shot from her right foot up the side of her leg.

"Uh-oh," she said. "You have a broken arm, and I think I've twisted my ankle. Great."

Marco sat down beside Maria and gingerly inspected her ankle in the dim light. "It's already starting to swell," he told her. Maria started to take her shoe off to have a closer look. "No," Marco said, stopping her. "If you keep your shoe on, it won't swell as much."

Maria was suddenly angry. "Marco," she said, "riding that stallion was about the dumbest thing you have ever done."

Marco just sat there, looking down at the ground.

"I was only trying to help find Munch-Munch," he finally said.

"Yeah, well, you nearly got us killed by disobeying Papa."

"I'm sorry." Marco shifted his weight uncomfortably and winced with pain.

At the sight of her brother's aching arm, Maria's anger softened. For the moment anyway.

Lowering her voice she said, "I know, I know." She paused, trying to think of how she and Marco could patch themselves up. She lifted the backpack onto her lap and opened it.

"What are you looking for?" Marco asked as she rummaged through the bag.

"Something for your arm," Maria answered "Look, here's one of those crazy bandannas you and Jake are always wearing. It might work."

"Yeah," Marco answered in a voice meant to sound like a rough cowboy. "They come in handy when we're ridin' the trails."

"Well," said Maria, "it will make a perfect sling. Turn around and let me tie it around your neck."

Marco hesitated. "You should use that for your ankle," he told her.

"I think your arm's in worse shape," she replied. "Come on. It's getting dark. We can't talk about this all night." Marco awkwardly turned his body in the dust.

"You're going to have to tell me how to do this," Maria told him with a half smile. "You're the doctor here, you know." Marco gave her step-by-step instructions on how to fold the bandanna into a triangle, loop it under his arm, and tie it around his neck. "Marco," Maria said quietly as she tightened the knot, "I have no idea where we are. Lightning's got to be miles from here by now. What are we going to do?"

Marco put on his bravest smile. "We're going to stay together and ask God to show us what to do next," he said. He took Maria's hand in his and closed his eyes. Maria found it hard to stay angry with a praying brother. "Dear Lord, me and Maria are lost and don't know what to do. Help us trust You to take care of us. And show us how we can help each other. In Jesus' name, amen."

"Thanks for praying," said Maria gratefully. This brother who so often tried to show off how smart he was surprised her just as often with his gentle kindness.

"You helped me feel calmer." Still, Maria found herself wondering if God had really heard Marco's prayer. *God, do You see us? Why is this happening if You really care for us more than sparrows?*

The sun slipped away to light the other side of the world, and the blue darkness became blacker by the minute.

"Okay," said Marco with a new air of determination, his prayerful tone slipping away. "Let's think about what we've got here: no horse, no daylight, one broken arm, one twisted ankle." Maria recognized this as the voice Marco used whenever he wanted to assure her that everything would work out fine. He fished a small flashlight out of the backpack and began searching the ground around him. "Let me find a stick for you to lean on. We're going to need to find some shelter for the night. I doubt we can get back home tonight, unless we are rescued."

"Mama and Papa will be so worried!" Maria exclaimed. "And Jake and Joy—what will they think? What will they do?"

As if on cue, the sky answered with a brilliant flash of light. A few seconds later, a low rumble followed in the distance.

"That's lightning!" Marco said.

"The horse?" Maria asked hopefully.

"No, silly. In the sky," Marco said. "We've got to get out of the open before it starts to rain." He kicked at some undergrowth and pointed his flashlight at the ground. "This stick looks good," he said, holding the flashlight between his knees and bending over to pick it up with his good hand. "Try walking with—oops!" The flashlight slipped and hit the hard ground with a crack, but the light stayed bright. It rolled a few feet away from Marco and came to a stop at the base of a stubby tree.

"Come back here," Marco muttered, shuffling his way toward the light. But when he got there, he didn't pick it up right away. "Wow," he said softly.

"What is it?" asked Maria. She couldn't see anything but the small beam of light shining up near Marco's shoes.

Marco reached for a low-hanging branch and tugged at it. Something came off in his hands.

"It looks like that little bow Munch-Munch wears." There was worry in his voice. "And it looks pretty beat-up."

5

CAVE DWELLERS

Another streak of lightning sizzled its way across the night sky. This time the crack of thunder came right away, loud and close. Big, pelting raindrops began to fall. The twins tried to avoid the forked lightning by huddling near a jagged boulder.

"I want to go home!" Maria said, shivering in the dark and fingering Munch-Munch's tattered little bow.

Marco nodded. "I know, Maria. But with this storm going on, they might not find us until morning. But don't worry—God will take care of us. Let's try to make it over to that rockface." He pointed in the direction of the formation Maria had seen before the sun had set. "It's not far, and I'm sure we'll be more sheltered there than here."

"Good idea. Give me that stick," Maria said. "I can walk. You hold the flashlight."

Marco helped Maria get up and handed her the stick he had found. Shining the flashlight in front of them, he guided her toward the rocks. They tried to hurry, but between the darkness and Maria's swollen ankle, they couldn't move quickly enough to avoid the soaking rain. After what seemed like years, they finally reached the rockface.

"Hey! There's an opening here!" Marco shouted above the rain. His light revealed a wide crack between two rocks. Maria and her brother squeezed through and were surprised to find that the crack was actually an entrance to a dry cave.

"Thank goodness there are so many caves around this area," Marco said, shining the light around.

Shivering in the chill, Maria said, "Well, I'm thankful Joy gave me Papa's big coat to wear before we rode off. I'd be freezing to death right now if she hadn't."

Marco nodded. "We have some matches in the backpack and can make a fire tomorrow morning to warm ourselves, but it's really too dark—and wet—to gather firewood now. If we stay close together, will you be warm enough to make it through the night?"

"I th-think so," Maria answered, trying to keep her teeth from chattering. She sat down next to Marco and looked at Munch-Munch's yellow and red polka-dot bow. It was torn in one spot, and a few pieces of fur were stuck in it, as if it had been yanked off her head. "How did Munchy get way out here?" Maria wondered aloud. "You don't think someone *took* her, do you?"

"I sure hope not," he said. "Why would anyone toss away her bow like that? Not a good idea if you don't want evidence of your crime lying around!"

"What if it came off when she was trying to escape? She might be out in this storm! Marco, I'm so wor—*aaaack!*"

A wild sound of beating wings came into the cave and whooshed over Maria's head. She frantically covered her face and hair while Marco shone his light around. Something black was fluttering around near the ceiling.

"What's *that?*" Maria asked in fright.

"Oh," said Marco, his interest rising, "that's a bat! Don't worry," he assured her. "He won't hurt you. He's just coming in out of the rain. He'll sleep up high on the cave ceiling."

Maria snuggled down inside her dad's coat to get warm and to hide her face from the eerie-looking black bat. *First Munchy disappears. Then there's a runaway horse, then a twisted ankle, then rain, and now I'm going to have to be cavemates with a bat.* Maria sure didn't feel like God was taking care of her. Not at all. Maybe He only answered the prayers of people like Joy—people who were more confident and trusting and outgoing. Maybe God didn't notice her because she was too quiet and shy. She was just invisible to Him among the crowd of the billions of people on earth.

Marco reached into the backpack and pulled out two small packages.

"What's that?" Maria asked.

"Dinner," Marco replied, handing Maria a Ziploc bag filled with raisins, peanuts, and M&M's. "Gorp," Jake and Marco called this mixture. "Survival food," they'd informed their sisters whenever they restocked their emergency backpacks.

"Mmm," Maria answered, scooping a small handful of gorp into her mouth. "I'm starving." Then, her mouth full of chocolate and nuts, she mumbled, "Just so you know, I'm still mad at you."

Marco grinned. "You'll get over it. Hey, slow down there. Just eat a little. This is all the food we have."

The twins ate just enough to stop the gnawing in their stomachs. Then, using the backpack as a pillow and huddling together against the cold, they tried to go to sleep on the cave floor.

But sleep did not come easily for Maria. A question burned in her heart. "Marco," she asked sincerely, "if God cares about sparrows, why does He allow them to fall to the ground? I mean, how can I trust God when He didn't save us from getting hurt?"

Marco thought a minute and then answered carefully, "I think that since our world isn't perfect, sometimes bad things do happen, even to good people—like when Jake got accused of stealing that watch even though he didn't take it. God doesn't say a sparrow won't *fall,* but He promises to be *with* the sparrow and never, ever leave the tiny fellow alone. Sometimes God helps us by giving us what we want. But I think sometimes He helps us by getting us *through* hard times instead."

"Oh," said Maria quietly, thinking over Marco's words. *Maybe God does care. Maybe He is watching over me, just not in the way I thought He would.* She drifted to sleep, dreaming that her papa's big red jacket was God's loving arms wrapped around her. She was cozy and warm. His comfort was soft, like a favorite furry toy animal, and it tickled her neck…

Maria scratched behind her ear, and then came fully to her senses when she realized where she was— and that the furry sensation at the back of her neck wasn't a dream. The hair on her arms stood up like quills on a porcupine.

"Marco," she whispered desperately to her brother, whose back was turned toward her. "There's something behind me. What is it? I'm afraid to look."

Marco turned over sleepily, and then stopped still. Keeping his voice low, he said carefully, "Don't move, Maria. I think it's our yellow-eyed mystery beast. And it's staring right at me."

6

THE CREATURE RETURNS

B e still!" Marco said again. His voice came out in a squeaky whisper. "It's huge!"

Maria held her breath and was still, but the yellow-eyed furry creature was not. Once again it left them in a hurry, its gigantic dark shape leaping over the twins in the dark and trotting out of the cave into the dimness of the early morning.

Maria remained still as stone. Her racing heart was the only thing in her body that moved. Neither she nor her brother spoke for several seconds, too stunned to follow the animal.

Marco broke the tense silence, reaching out to touch his sister's arm. "You're shaking," he said.

Maria finally let her breath go in a long hiss. "Well yeah," she said. "I'm cold and I just had the fright of my life."

Marco stood up, the pain in his arm making him wince in the process. His hair stood up in all directions. He walked toward the mouth of the cave, cocked his head, and stepped outside. "Thank you, Lord!" Maria heard him exclaim.

"Why did you say that?" Maria called from inside.

"I can see a little pink ribbon of light in the east. Won't be long before we have some light and can figure out where we are!"

"What if that animal is a mountain lion or a cougar or something?" Maria said, worried.

"Well," answered Marco, "then I'll have a lot more to thank the Lord for. We could have been its breakfast."

"I hope he's not planning to save us for lunch. How big do you think it was?" asked Maria as she struggled to one foot and hobbled out to where Marco was standing.

"I'm not sure. But I'm almost positive it's the same animal that spooked Lightning yesterday."

Maria shivered. "Marco, I *really* hope they find us—*soon.*"

Marco put his good arm around her and squeezed. "Trust God, Maria. He'll take care of us. He always has and He always will. Besides, we're learning something from this."

"What?" she asked.

"We're learning to trust Him to care for us in different ways. He's helping us be brave."

"But I'm *not* brave! I'm scared to death."

"Being brave doesn't mean you don't feel scared," Marco said wisely. "Actually, you can only be brave if you *are* afraid. Being brave means that *when* you are scared, you don't panic. You trust God for the courage to do whatever you have to do even when you're afraid."

"Oh," Maria answered thoughtfully. "I never thought about it that way."

"To tell you the truth, I hadn't either. Not before Papa explained it like that," Marco said.

Marco began to hum a golden oldies song that Mrs. Bigsley liked to sing on summer mornings. To cheer up Maria, he began to sing the words aloud. "Here comes the sun, da-da-da-da-da, and I say, 'It's all right...'"

Maria hummed along as she gazed toward the horizon where the morning sun was painting the sky the color of a ripe watermelon. In the soft light of dawn the twins checked out the land around them. The ground in front of the cave was sandy and firm with bits of cactus and scrub brush plants scattered about like tufts of short, stubby green hair. Behind them and to the west were more rocky cliff formations. Below the western mountains and to the south were dense forests that went on and on for as far as their eyes could see.

This region of Arizona had a little bit of every kind of land, it seemed to Maria: desert, rocks, mountains, and huge areas of forest as well, all within a short distance of each other.

"You know what Dad says about this place," Maria said.

"Yep," said Marco.

Then together they repeated, "If you don't like the land around you, walk five feet in any direction."

"Speaking of directions," Maria said, leaning against a rock to take the weight off her sore ankle, "which way do you suppose is home?"

Marco pointed west, then south. "It's got to be

one of those two directions since the horse took us through the woods before plopping us here. But who knows which one, or how far Lightning took us? With your bum foot and my broken arm, I don't think we should try to chance finding our way home."

Maria nodded, "I know. At least here we have shelter and—look!—there's a stream. Water!"

Marco responded with a slow smile, then pulled a box of matches out of the backpack. "I'll see if I can find some dry kindling somewhere under that rock ledge, and we'll make a fire in front of the cave. It will keep us warm, and if we fan the smoke with our coats, maybe someone will see it."

"Good idea," Maria agreed.

"Maria, if you can, hobble over to the stream and fill this pan with water. We'll boil it for hot chocolate."

"You packed a pan? And hot chocolate?" Maria asked, her eyes wide.

Marco nodded. "Yep, I always stash four packets of powdered hot chocolate."

"I promise, I will *never* make fun of you and your backpack ever again," Maria said, her spirits rising with the thought of sipping something warm and chocolaty on this crisp, cold morning. "But just so you know, I'm still mad at you."

She felt a little guilty for holding a grudge though, so she asked, "How's your arm doing?"

Marco rubbed it gently. "It hurts pretty bad and it's black and blue. See?"

Maria patted his good arm comfortingly. A deep purple bruise started just above Marco's elbow and continued up to just below his shoulder. "I don't think it's broken in two," Marco continued with the authority of a doctor. "Most likely it's a small fracture, surrounded by multiple contusions."

Maria just nodded. Marco prided himself on his first-aid knowledge. He must have read *The American Red Cross First Aid and Safety Handbook* seven times this past summer, and he was always quoting from it at the oddest times. They'd be having dinner as a family, talking about school or the weather, and Marco would get a faraway look in his eyes and say something like, "Did you know that the liver is one of the most important organs, cleansing toxins out of the body every minute of the day?"

To which Maria would say, "Please, Marco, we are eating."

And her mother would say, "Marco, you're so smart! You are going to be a doctor someday and make your mama so proud!"

And her papa would say, "Please, son, pass the beans—without liver."

Marco looked down at Maria's foot. "How's your ankle there?"

"Sore," said Maria. "But I can put a little weight on it this morning. I think I'll be fine if I just move slowly."

"Take your time," Marco said. "I'm going to empty out the backpack and use it to carry kindling and wood. With only one arm, I'll need it."

Maria waited for Marco to bring her the pan. Then she carefully step-hopped her way down to the edge of the stream. *I wonder how Mama and Papa are this morning? I bet they are really worried. Please, God, take care of them, too. And protect little Munchy, wherever she is.*

Maria knelt down on one knee and dipped the shiny pan into the water to fill it. She was startled to see her own reflection so clearly in the little pool of water where the stream was dammed up by a beaver's abandoned home. She noticed how dirty her face was, and her long black hair, which was usually combed smooth or neatly braided, hung in wild tangles over her shoulders. "Oh, well," Maria said to herself. "I'm not out here to win a beauty contest." Suddenly another reflection joined hers, and Maria stiffened.

It was an enormous gray-and-white wolf with searching yellow eyes.

"Dear Lord," she whispered. "Help me."

7
DOG IN WOLF'S CLOTHING

Maria slowly turned around to face the beautiful, fearsome creature.

She stood very still, and then noticed that the wolf seemed much more like a house dog than a wild animal. It blinked its yellow eyes and wandered over to get a drink of water. Then it came toward Maria, wagging its tail as if it wanted to be petted.

"Good puppy," Maria said, trying to keep her voice low and calm as the wolf approached her and sat down on its haunches.

Carefully, Maria reached out to pet the gray wolf, which nuzzled her jeans, begging for a better scratch between its ears. Then it dropped to the ground and rolled over, waiting for Maria to pet its white tummy. When she did just that, the wolf reached around to lick her hands and face. Flipping back over onto its feet, it began sniffing at her jacket and pawing one of her pockets.

"Stop, boy!" Maria said, laughing out loud.

"Maria!" It was Marco running toward her from the woods, a big stick in his hand poised to scare off the wild animal.

"No, Marco!" Maria yelled back. "It's okay! He's a friendly wolf!"

"A *what?*" Marco said as he neared the unbelievable scene near the water's edge.

"It's a friendly wolf. Look!" Maria petted the huge animal as he leaned on her legs, nuzzling her elbow with his nose.

"No way…" was all Marco could say as he dropped the firewood to the ground and walked over to get a closer look at the gentle, doglike wolf.

"What should we call him?" Maria asked.

"How about 'Spot'?" Marco said scratching the animal between its ears.

"No," Maria answered. "I think we should call him 'Lobo.'"

"The Spanish word for 'wolf.' Nice," Marco said.

Lobo ignored Marco's attention and sniffed at Maria's hands and jacket pocket again. The wolf-dog whined and began to paw at Maria, almost knocking her over. "Whoa, Lobo—what do you want in there?" she asked. Maria reached into her pocket and remembered that she had tucked Munchy's bow in there the night before. Drawing it out, she didn't even have the chance to look at it before Lobo lunged, snatching the bow out of her hands and dashing away.

"Hey! Wait a minute!" Maria began. But Lobo was already gone.

8

FREEDOM IN FORGIVENESS

"Brrrrr," Maria said as she finished scooping the saucepan full of cold spring water. "This water is freezing, and so am I. Did you find firewood?"

"Yep," Marco said, nodding and walking toward the backpack stuffed with wood. He leaned over to pick it up carefully with one arm and said, "Bring the water back to the cave. I'll need you to help me strike the match and start the fire since I'm working as a one-armed man today."

"A man? So you've spent one night in the wild and now you're a *man?*" Maria teased.

Marco shrugged off her comment and heaved at the bag full of firewood. "I'm taking care of you, aren't I?"

"Yeah," Maria answered. "Right after you nearly killed me."

"Oh, come *on, Maria,*" Marco answered gruffly. "Get over it already and quit reminding me! Haven't you ever made a teensy mistake?"

"Yes," admitted Maria.

"Well then, why don't you forgive me and forget it?"

"Because I've made teensy mistakes. The mistake you made is *huge.*"

"With God sin is sin, no matter how small or big. And He forgives us as soon as we say we were wrong and ask Him to."

"But I'm not God," Maria said.

"Thank goodness," Marco answered. "Or the whole human race would be in a heap of trouble. And everybody on the earth who ever made a wrong choice would be sittin' in the corner forever."

Maria limped quietly behind Marco toward the cave, gingerly trying not to put too much weight on her foot.

"That hurt," she said aloud.

"Your ankle?" Marco asked. "You okay?"

"No," she said, "what you just said hurt."

They were at the cave now, and Maria set the pan down, trying not to spill the water. Standing up and looking Marco in the eye, she took a deep breath and said, "I forgive you for talking me into getting on that stallion. Really, I think I'm just as mad at myself for refusing to obey Papa too. I'm a part of getting us in this mess."

"I really am sorry," Marco said extra pitifully, pushing his bottom lip out like an enormously sad toddler.

Maria laughed aloud. "Me too."

Her heart felt strangely light, as if a load had been lifted from it and was now floating toward heaven. *So this is what forgiveness feels like,* she thought to herself. Then she remembered that once, when she was a little girl, her mother had told her, "Maria, forgiveness is like deciding to set a prisoner free and then finding out that the prisoner was you." She hadn't understood her mother's words at the time, but now, for the first time she did. In spite of all that had happened to her since yesterday afternoon, she suddenly knew God was here. He did care about her, and He was teaching her His ways.

9
SMOKE SIGNALS

It took a few tries and lots of blowing and huffing and match striking, but finally Marco and Maria had a respectable fire going. Even the driest wood Marco could find still had a little dampness from last night's rain, and smoke rose above the flames. Maria put the pan of water in the middle of the small fire until it was hot enough to pour into the empty canteen Marco had packed along.

Carefully, Maria poured the contents of two cocoa mix packets into the canteen—another blessed backpack item—then tightened the lid and shook it up.

Next she took the lid, put the canteen to her lips and swallowed the sweet hot liquid eagerly. Maria closed her eyes and said, "Mmmmm. It tastes like a melted Hershey's Bar mixed with fresh cream! I don't know if I've ever tasted anything better!"

Marco reached for the canteen and sipped. "Things always taste better outdoors."

"I would have liked having Lobo as a pet," Maria said out of the blue. She wondered why the animal had been so interested in Munchy's bow and where he had run off with it.

"A *pet?*" Marco asked, bursting into laughter. He handed the canteen back to Maria and wiped a dribble of hot chocolate off his chin. "Oh, yeah. I'm sure Mama would just love to have a wolf lying around the house, eating legs off of her furniture, gnawing his way through the dining room wall…"

"He would have made a nice *outside* pet!" Maria insisted. "I bet he'll come back again, don't you? He had such a sweet, baby wolfie face—"

"If he shows up," Marco interrupted, "Don't tell him he has a 'sweet, baby wolfie' face. He's a strong, fierce, wild animal. Besides, he probably has a home around here somewhere."

Home.

How Maria longed for that right now. Home where her mother kept a nice, neat house and steaming hot *menudo,* her favorite Mexican stew, simmering on the stove. Home where her papa would give her nightly bear hugs. Home where her best friend was coping with worry and a broken heart. Poor Joy—first Munchy disappeared, and now she and Marco were lost as well.

Maria stared into the fire. Lost. What if they were never found? Could they ever get back on their own? She focused on the trail of smoke winding upward from the wet wood.

"Marco," said Maria. "Maybe we'd better try to make some of those smoke signals you talked about."

"Right." Marco took off his jacket, and together he and Maria waved it over the fire, sending puffs of smoke up and over the canyon and forest.

"There," said Marco after several minutes. "If someone is looking for us, that should give them a clue. I'm counting on Jake to figure it out. We talked about this."

"Talked about what?" asked Maria.

"Talked about what to do if we ever got lost.

Talked about making smoke signals and such. You have to be prepared for anything you know. That's what the Boy Scouts say."

Maria took a long sip of hot chocolate and a handful of the last bit of gorp. Marco was just the calm, cool friend she needed right now to keep her from growing afraid.

The soft sound of padding feet coming up from the stream caught Maria's attention, and she turned.

"Lobo!" she cried.

"Well, he did come back then," Marco said. "What's that he's got in his mouth?"

"It looks like a rag," Maria said. "A yellow rag."

Marco stood slowly as Lobo dragged the cloth through the dirt toward the little campfire. "That's no rag, Maria," he said softly. "It's a Camp Wanna Banana T-shirt."

Lobo dropped the dirty shirt, and Marco bent to pick it up. It was torn down the back, and the right sleeve was covered in brownish red stains. "It looks like it's got a lot of blood on it."

Maria covered her mouth with her hands. "Munchy," she whispered.

1 0

HUNTER AND HUNTED

The sun was fully visible now and warmed Maria's back. Lobo stretched himself in front of the fire while the twins studied Munch-Munch's Camp Wanna Banana shirt. Worry for the lost little monkey kept Maria cold in spite of the higher temperatures.

"Marco, we've got to do something. She must be hurt really bad. Who would want to hurt her?"

"It might not be a who, but a what," Marco said, taking a close look at the ripped-up sleeve. "These tears could be claw marks. Maybe an animal got after her."

"Do you think Lobo knows where she is?" Maria wondered. She looked over at the relaxed dog.

Suddenly a rabbit hopped into view. As Maria screamed, "No, Lobo!" the wolf took off toward the rabbit, grabbed it with his strong jaws and broke its neck. Then the wolf proudly laid the dead prey at Maria's feet. He looked up at her expectantly, as if waiting for her to praise him.

Tears stung Maria's eyes. "Look what Lobo did to this poor little rabbit!"

Marco was matter-of-fact. "Maria, that's how animals survive in the wilderness. It seems sad to you, but Lobo may have just handed us our breakfast."

"No *way!*" shouted Maria. "I am *not* going to eat Bugs Bunny for breakfast."

Marco shook his head and lifted the rabbit by its ears. Maria took a wobbly step backward. "Well, I'm taking the rabbit down and tying it to a rock in the stream so it will stay cold," Marco announced, "in case we have to cook it later! I'm also going to see if Lobo left any tracks. The ground is soft from last night's rain, and if Munchy was anywhere near her shirt, Lobo's prints might lead me to her."

"You?" Maria asked, suddenly fearful that Marco would leave her alone.

"You're in no shape to walk," he said. "And besides, we need someone to keep the fire and smoke signals going. It looks like Lobo might stay here with you now." Lobo was lying by the fire again, sound asleep now. "He's had a busy morning."

"Okay," Maria said weakly. "Please don't be gone long."

Marco soon disappeared from view with the limp rabbit. Maria moved close to Lobo and surveyed the land and woods around her, hoping to see a sign of someone coming to rescue them and take them home. She rubbed Lobo's ears, letting her hand move down his neck.

What was that?

Buried under Lobo's thick, silvery coat was a collar. A small ID tag was attached to it. Maria gazed at the small coin-shaped piece of metal.

"Animal Haven Ranch, Shadow Rock, Arizona," Maria read aloud. "That's weird," Maria said. "Do you belong to a *ranch* for wolves?" She had never heard of anything like it, but it could explain why the animal was so tame. Oh how she wished for a pet like him! But now it appeared he belonged to someone else.

Marco had been gone about an hour when Maria suddenly had an awful thought. She looked at Lobo's stomach, rising and falling with each deep, sleepy breath. Lobo had killed a rabbit. The clues—a wolf that kills small animals, a missing small monkey…

"Lobo," said Maria aloud, her thoughts making her sick at heart, "you don't eat monkeys, do you?"

Lobo jerked suddenly and awoke, his nostrils flaring.

"Easy, boy," Maria said as calmly as she could manage. "I didn't mean anything—" But Lobo bared his sharp teeth, growling at Maria. The hair on his back stood straight up as he barked fiercely.

Before Maria could blink, Lobo sprang past in a terrifying lunge. *Not another poor rabbit,* Maria thought. Then she whipped her head around and saw a sight that made her heart leap into her throat.

11

SURPRISE ATTACK!

E ven in the glare of the sun Maria could make out the towering shape clearly. It was blackish brown with powerful claws. A bear!

Maria screamed and froze. *Run!* she thought to herself, but for a long moment she couldn't move. *Snap out of it!* She fumbled for her walking stick. Could she make it to the cave before the bear did? She was pretty sure he couldn't fit through the small opening. Or could he? Forgetting the walking stick, she began to crawl as quickly as she could toward the mouth of the cave.

Lobo was barking—a deep, gruff sound Maria had not heard before. She glanced at the animals over her shoulder. The wolf's bark only angered the outraged bear who, with one quick swipe of its heavy paw, left a long, bleeding scrape down Lobo's back.

The wolf whimpered, then rose up in equal fury, knocking the bear's paw away with his huge head. The bear started to swipe with his other arm, but Lobo caught the bear's big forearm with his teeth and bit down hard before the claws could dig into his skin. In a shock of pain, the bear growled, his open mouth revealing sharp white teeth. For a few seconds, the bear acted as though it might counterattack, then he paused and backed away, finally turning and running across the ground toward the safety of the forest, a loping ball of dark fur.

Lobo stood at attention, guarding, until the bear was out of sight. Then, whimpering, he slowly limped into the cave, shaking and licking his wound.

"Lobo!" Maria yelled.

"Mar-iiii-aaa! Maaaaaar-co!" a girl's voiced called from somewhere near the edge of the woods. "Mar-iiii-aaa! Maaaaaar-co!"

Maria saw Jake and Joy, riding on Brick, galloping toward them.

"Jake! Joy!" Maria called. "Over here!"

In a whirl of dirt around the clopping of four hooves, the twins rode quickly to the mouth of the cave where Maria sat. Joy was talking into one of the camp's high-powered walkie-talkies. "We found them! They're okay! We're at the base of Black Bear Cliff."

"Whoa, boy," Jake said, clicking his tongue and pulling up on Brick's reins. As soon as the horse came to a halt, Jake jumped off and spoke to Maria in a rush of relief and concern. "Hey, the whole town's been out looking for you! Are you okay? Your ankle's hurt. Where's Marco?"

"We found some clues about Munchy, and Marco went to check them out," Maria explained. Joy's eyes went wide, and Maria wasn't sure how much to tell. She wanted Joy to be hopeful, but she didn't know if Munch-Munch was okay. She looked around casually to see where Munch-Munch's T-shirt was—under the backpack. She hoped Joy wouldn't see it. "He should be back soon, I think," she said, changing the subject. "Where are we? How did you find us?"

"This is Black Bear Cliff. Bears like to hibernate in that cave for the winter. Mr. Fields drove our science class in the school bus over here once for a field trip. Joy and I were scoping out the area from the Tree Top Meeting House this morning and saw your smoke signals." Jake turned to Joy, "I told you Marco would think of that!"

"Maria!" Marco's voice came up from the direction of the stream, and he soon appeared from behind some brush.

"Marco, Jake and Joy are here!" Maria called back. A bright smile lit up Marco's face.

"Did you find anything?" Maria and Joy asked at the same time.

Marco carried something very small in his hands, and he looked down at it, his smile disappearing. "Just her bow," Marco said. "Lobo must have set it down when he went back to get the shirt. If Munchy was there before, she's gone now."

"What shirt?" Joy asked, alarmed. "And who's Lobo?"

"He's my new pet wolf," Maria said. "Joy, don't be frightened, but I have to go see him. I think he may be hurt pretty badly."

"Huh? What?" Joy started to ask, then she caught sight of the enormous gray creature coming out of the cave, blood dripping from the side of its neck— and she screamed.

12

RESCUE AND WORRY

There now," Maria said soothingly as she held Lobo's head in her lap. She explained about the wolf and about the bear attack and also about the fact that Lobo turned out to be tame—at least to humans.

"That bear must have smelled the rabbit that Lobo got and came looking for it," Marco suggested. "Or maybe the blood on the T-sh—" he clapped his hand over his mouth, and looked at Joy.

"What are you talking about?" Joy asked in a near whisper, as if she wasn't sure she wanted to know.

Maria and Marco told their friends everything they knew. Joy held Munch-Munch's bow and shirt close to her chest and began to cry softly.

Maria put her arm around Joy while Jake and Marco went down to the spring to get some clean water to pour over Lobo's leg. When they got back they cleaned the wound, which fortunately was not too deep, and covered it with the red bandanna Jake kept in his survival pack. It matched Marco's sling.

"Hey partner," Marco said, patting the calm wolf on its rump. "Now you look like a real cow-dog."

Lobo licked Joy's hand in response. "Oh, Maria," she sniffed. "He's soooo sweet."

"I know," said Maria. "Now all I have to do is convince Mama of that!"

"Oh," Joy said, "she'll be so glad to see you two, I think she might just give you anything you want today!"

"How *are* my parents?" Maria asked.

"Terribly worried," answered Joy. "But they prayed and trusted God to care for you all through the night last night. Your dad and mine and several other men from Tall Pines looked for you as best they could. But it got so dark, and the storm forced them to turn back."

Jake nodded and then added, "Our mom and Joy and I stayed with your mama last night, and of course, she couldn't sleep a wink. She kept saying, 'The Lord will take care of my bambinos' over and over again as she paced the living room."

Marco reached over for Maria's hand and patted it. "Mama was right."

Maria nodded and looked up at Joy. "God takes care of His fallen sparrows, even though one of them has a broken wing and one has a sore foot."

"I sure hope He's taking care of the one who's still missing," Joy said quietly, looking at Munchy's bow.

Maria heard the sound of a jeep coming over the desert ground from somewhere around the cliffs. Once the jeep screeched to a halt, Señor and Señora Garcia and Mr. Fields, the kids' science teacher, jumped out and ran toward Marco and Maria.

There were shouts of joy and hugs and tears of gratitude for God's protection, mixed with looks of sympathy for Marco's arm and Maria's sore ankle.

Maria excitedly told the story of how the wolf had saved her life by fighting off the angry, hungry bear. Señora Garcia looked over at Lobo, who was snuggling his huge head on Maria's lap. Maria looked up from where she was sitting on the ground by the crackling fire, stroking the giant animal gently, and asked, "Can I keep him?"

Señora Garcia laughed and walked over to kiss her daughter, for the seventh time. "If your papa can build a big pen for him and we can find out for sure that he is safe to keep as a pet, I'll think about it. But only because he saved your life!"

"It looks like we'll also have to be sure he doesn't belong to someone else," said Mr. Fields, who was not only the twins' science teacher, but also the camp nature counselor and friend to both families. He had been rubbing Lobo's neck. "It looks like an ID tag."

"I know," Maria said sadly. "It says, 'Animal Haven Ranch.'"

"Really now?" said Mr. Fields, examining the tag. "That's not far from here. It's a ranch built by a young couple in our church to protect and take care of exotic pets. Often the owners of exotics turn out not to be able to care for their pets."

"What's an exotic pet?" Joy asked.

"Well," Mr. Fields answered, "an exotic pet is just about any kind of animal that isn't your everyday dog, cat, bird, or hamster. For example, Lobo here is a hybrid wolf-dog."

"A harebrained wolf-dog?" Jake asked with rising interest.

Mr. Fields chuckled. "No, Jake. A *hybrid* dog. That's one who has a dog and a wolf for parents. The two breeds mate and produce a gentler doglike wolf. In fact, I'm guessing that Lobo is probably half malamute."

"Really?" asked Maria. "What's a malamute?

"It's a large dog used for pulling sleds through heavy snow," Mr. Fields said as he walked over to pet Lobo's huge sleeping form. "We'll need to take him back to the ranch. Trevor, the owner, is a vet. He'll probably want to make sure that scratch doesn't get infected." Then turning to Señor Garcia, he said, "Most of the animals at Animal Haven are waiting to be adopted by good folks who will care for them."

"Aren't these animals dangerous?" Señor Garcia asked.

"None of the ones that are up for adoption anyway," said Mr. Fields. Looking at Lobo who was sleeping like a giant puppy, he added, "I'd guess this fellow's been loved by humans for a long time. Even full blood wolves don't attack humans in the wild. It's beef on four hooves that they go after—cattle."

"So what do sled dogs eat?" Señora Garcia asked, her black eyes wide.

"Well," said Mr. Fields, "I once had a friend who had a malamute when I was in college in Alaska. As I recall, the dog was especially fond of the legs on the kitchen table."

Señora Garcia's mouth dropped open, and everyone laughed. Everyone except Maria, who was pondering an awful possibility. *Please God,* she prayed, but not aloud, *don't let Munchy be wolf food right now.*

13

MYSTERIES UNRAVELED

Señor Garcia volunteered to ride Brick back to Camp, since he knew the way through the woods. He hoped to find the missing stallion on his way. Mr. Fields loaded everyone else up in the jeep, drove to town, and dropped Señora Garcia, Jake, and Marco off at Dr. Benton's in town to get x-rays of Marco's arm.

"Señora Garcia," Mr. Fields said as Maria's mother and Marco exited the jeep, "do you mind if I take Joy and Maria up to Animal Haven Ranch? Trevor can treat those scratches. If Lobo checks out, I can see if he's up for adoption."

Señora Garcia smiled weakly and nodded, putting her arm around Marco and blowing Maria a kiss. Maria knew her mama probably just wanted to go somewhere quiet to collapse and cry and say a prayer of thanks now that her children were safe. Maria's heart almost ached with love for her mother right now. *Who cares if she's a little picky about the house?* she thought to herself. *She's my precious* mamacita *(little mama) and I love her.*

Maria looked over at Lobo, who was licking his wound. Though Maria wanted very much to adopt Lobo, she had to admit she felt confused about it now. How could she love a wolf-dog that might have munched Munch-Munch for breakfast?

The ride up to Animal Haven Ranch didn't take long. The jeep's wheels made a popping sound as they rolled over the gravel drive in front of the entry to the ranch.

A handsome man with straw-colored hair, wearing blue jeans and boots and a denim shirt, walked out the metal gate to greet the visitors. Behind him was a pretty lady dressed in a loose-fitting denim jumper. Her short, curly black hair waved in the breeze under her cowboy hat.

"Hi, Jim!" the man called to Mr. Fields, waving his hand as he spoke. "What brings you this way?"

At the sound of the man's voice, Lobo jumped out of the jeep and ran toward the couple. "Zeb!" the woman said with surprise, trying to keep her balance as the huge animal leaned on her, begging to have his ears scratched. "Where have you been, you bad boy?"

Maria's heart fell. It sounded like Lobo had another home already—and another name.

"Trevor and Tori," Mr. Fields said, "meet Joy and Maria. And it looks like you already know our wolf-dog friend here."

"Yes," laughed Trevor. "Zeb dug under that pen over there a few days ago," he explained, pointing toward a huge dog pen up the hill from where they were standing. "Tori's been worried about him ever since. How'd you find him?"

Mr. Fields told the story while Joy and Maria looked around. There were big pens scattered every-where. One contained an ostrich, the other a potbel-lied pig, the other a cougar—it was like Old MacDonald's *Zoo!*

"Of course, it's not as if we don't have plenty of animals for Tori to worry after, even without Zeb. But of course Zeb isn't up for adoption. He's Tori's baby," Trevor commented as he reached over to hug his wife and pet the jumping, lapping animal. "We've got at least three hybrid wolves, two wildcats, a boa constrictor and—"

"Let me guess," Mr. Fields interrupted. "A partridge in a pear tree?"

"Just about." Trevor laughed again. "In fact this morning we had a horse wander up lookin' for a drink of water and some fresh oats."

"Oh?" Mr. Fields asked.

"Yep," Tori said. "A midnight black stallion. Beautiful horse. Sure is a feisty fellow though."

"Yeah," Maria said rubbing her ankle. "Tell me about it."

"You know him? Well, how about that!" Trevor said. "You got some challenge on your hands, I gotta tell ya."

Maria grimaced again. "My *dad's* got some challenge on his hands. I, personally, will not be riding Lightning for a very long time."

Tori nodded and laughed. "I think you'd like what

we found yesterday while we were out looking for
Zeb. Come on back to the nursery and see."

"The nursery?" Maria asked.

"Yes," said Tori. She gently patted her round
stomach as she led the girls down the hall of their
ranch style house to a bedroom. "I'm going to have a
baby in a few months, so we already started fixing up
the nursery. But I didn't expect to have something to
put in the crib this soon!"

The girls tiptoed quietly into the pastel bedroom
and peeked inside the white wicker baby bed. There,
asleep under a pale blue blanket, was a tiny form with
soft black hair on its head. And neck. And arms!

14

ROCK-A-BYE *WHAT?*

"M unch-Munch!" Joy cried, reaching for her pet, tears of happiness welling in her eyes. Munch-Munch sat up slowly, blinking her eyes in an effort to wake up. Her right arm was bandaged, and she whimpered slightly as Joy stroked her tenderly.

Tori looked at the monkey and Joy in surprise. "So you *know* our hairy little visitor?"

Joy couldn't speak through her tears; she could only nod. Maria explained for her, "This is the little critter who started this whole crazy adventure. When she disappeared, we went in search of her and that's how we ended up lost!"

Tori smiled and then explained, "We found this little spider monkey a short way down the river from Black Bear Cliff, huddled under a tree."

Just then, Lobo made his way into the bedroom, nosing his head between Maria and Joy for a look at the monkey. At the sight of the wolf, Munch-Munch made a weak but happy "chee-chee" noise and reached out to touch his nose.

Lobo gently licked the monkey's hand. Tori laughed, "This gentle wolf-dog always did love little animals. He played with cats and kittens and puppies the way a child plays with dolls. From the way these two are going on with each other, Munchy and Zeb probably have met before."

Joy wiped her cheek with the back of her hand and sniffed before saying, "Do you think Munchy went off to play with Lobo that day Maria and I were talking at the Banana Bash Zone?"

As if in answer to Joy's question, Munchy let herself down from Joy's arms onto Lobo's back, holding on to the wolf-dog's neck as if he were a horse. Lobo obliged by taking Munchy on a "wolfie ride" around the house.

"So that's how Munch-Munch got this far away from camp! She must have 'ridden' Lobo through the woods!" Maria exclaimed. "I bet that's how she lost her bow in the scrub brush, too."

Tori laughed. "You must be right. There's no other way a little monkey could have made it so far from Camp Wanna Banana so fast without—er, uh—help." Tori gave the large animal a friendly hug and then, turning to Maria, said, "So you've been calling Zeb 'Lobo,' huh?"

Maria nodded, then, not wanting to cry, quickly changed the subject. "How did Munchy get hurt?"

"Trevor thinks she must have gotten in a tussle with a bobcat," Tori said. "My guess is that the only thing that saved Munch-Munch from being bobcat chow was her friendship with Zeb."

"Lobo must have saved Munch-Munch from the bobcat the way he saved Maria from the bear!" Joy exclaimed. She reached to scratch the dog's ears and said, "What a good boy you are!"

Maria blinked back tears. *Yes, what a good boy you are. Too bad you can never be mine since you belong to Tori—and she loves you so much.*

15

HIS EYE IS ON THE SPARROW

T he sun made the autumn trees in Tall Pine City Park sparkle like branches full of rubies and sapphires and diamonds.

"You nervous?" Joy asked.

"A little," admitted Maria.

Just then the park flooded with the bass tones of a man's voice coming from speakers all over the park. "All those who entered the Tall Pines Pet Show, please line up for the awards ceremony."

Joy held Munch-Munch in her arms as she walked

toward the show booth. Today Munchy was dressed like a little doll in a jumper of red velvet and lace with a matching bow clipped to her hairy little brown head. Munchy's arm was healing well, and only a tiny white bandage covered it now. Tori had taken great care of Munchy and made Joy and Maria promise to bring her up to Animal Haven for a visit and a fresh banana now and then.

Maria followed closely behind Joy, with Lobo on a dog leash at her side. She had spent the morning washing, drying, and combing Lobo's beautiful coat of dark silver and snow white until it shone. Though he still belonged to Trevor and Tori, they'd allowed Maria to walk and show him in the Tall Pines Pet Show. Maria still couldn't bring herself to call him Zeb. He would always be Lobo to her.

That morning at the park before the show, even Maria's mother had said, "He is a handsome dog, Maria. *Muy bonito!*"

The balding announcer—dressed quite formally in a black tuxedo and bow tie—walked to the stage and stood in front of the microphone, clearing his throat. "And now, ladies and gentlemen, dogs and cats, parakeets and boa constrictors, and all God's critters gathered here: the moment you've all been waiting for!"

He triumphantly pulled a crisp, white card out of an envelope and read, "Our judges have picked winners in many categories. First, the winner of the Highest Jumper Award: Jake Bigsley and Warty the toad!"

Maria and Joy grinned as Jake and Marco pulled Warty, Jake's favorite toad, out of a bucket and took turns holding him up in the air for all to see. Marco's arm was still in a sling. Marco had been correct; he'd suffered a small fracture in the middle of his upper arm, where the doctor could not put a cast. But Marco was tough and healing quickly. Maria's twisted ankle had completely healed within three days after the rescue.

The announcer gave trophies for Most Colorful Pet (a parrot), Prettiest Pet (a longhaired Siamese cat), and Slimiest Pet (a grass snake).

"Cutest Pet," the announcer said with a broad smile, "goes to Tall Pine's favorite mischievous monkey—Munch-Munch Bigsley!"

Munchy jumped down from Joy's arms at the sound of her name and ran up on stage. Before the announcer knew what was happening, Munch-Munch had wrapped herself around his head, her tiny fingers quickly removing the balding man's glasses. The crowd went wild when Munch-Munch held the man's glasses up to her face and peered out. The lenses made the monkey's eyes look the size of Ping-Pong balls. The more Munchy looked and stared at the audience with intense curiosity, the more they laughed.

Even the announcer began to chuckle. "Perhaps we should have given Munch-Munch the Curious George Award!"

Joy had to come on stage and pry the glasses out of Munchy's naughty hands. "Sorry," Joy apologized to the man, and then she scolded the monkey, trying not to grin as she did so.

After the laughter died down, the announcer grew serious. "The next prize is perhaps the most important award of all. It goes to a pet that helped protect someone's life. Many of you have heard the story of how a lone wolf saved one of Tall Pine's young ladies from the claws of a black bear. The Bravest Pet award goes to Lobo, the wolf-dog, belonging to Maria Garcia!"

Maria blinked and looked over at Trevor and Tori, who were nodding and smiling. Had the announcer said, *"belonging to Maria Garcia?"* It must have been a mistake. Maria looked up at the judge and said, "Sir, I'm just showing the dog for Trevor and Tori. His name is Zeb, and he belongs to them."

The judge said, "Hmm…let me check my notes. Ah, yes! There's a note from the owners here. It says, 'We would like to give this beautiful wolf-dog, Zeb, to the brave and wonderful Maria Garcia, who is leading him in the pet show today. She's also given him a new name, Lobo, which we think fits him perfectly."

Just then Tori and Trevor came out of the clapping crowd to hug the bewildered but happy Maria. "Won't you miss him?" Maria asked Tori.

"Of course we will," she answered. Then patting her rounded belly, Tori said, "But very soon, I'm going to have my hands very full with our new baby. And I think Lobo will get the best care and attention from you, Maria. He obviously loves you! So we talked to your parents, and they agreed that you could have him."

Gratitude welled up like spring flowers in Maria's heart—for Lobo, for Trevor and Tori's generosity, for her parents' love, and most of all, for a God who always cared about her, even though sometimes she couldn't understand what He was doing.

Lobo licked Maria's hand. Trevor motioned for Maria to continue as he and Tori stepped back into the crowd. Maria whispered, "Thank you," to the kind couple, then turned and proudly walked Lobo to the stage. He obeyed like a champion, following close to her heels. The crowd ooohed and ahhhed at the beautiful, enormous animal, and everyone wanted to reach out and pet his thick, soft, silvery coat.

Maria reached for the trophy with one hand and leaned down to hug the neck of her new, much-beloved pet. She could still feel the scab left by the claw of the black bear, buried beneath the deep fur on Lobo's neck. On their way back to where the contestants were standing around in a circle, a bird began chirping in a tree branch above them. Its voice was sweet and high and clear.

"What's that?" Maria asked as she rejoined Joy, who was looking up at the source of the tweeting sound.

"I believe it's a sparrow," Joy replied.

A small black bird flittered from branch to branch

in a flurry of feathers and chirps. "I believe you're right," Maria said with a slow, knowing smile. "It's the kind of ordinary bird that may never win a pet show, but a bird God cares about just the same."

"The way He cares about you," said Joy, hugging her friend tightly. "And me."

THE TWIBLINGS' ACTIVITY PAGES

Always ask an adult to help you
with these crafts and recipes!

EXOTIC PET WORD SEARCH

Circle the exotic pet names in the following word puzzle. Be sure to look in all directions!

U	E	S	I	O	T	R	O	T
K	F	O	S	Y	I	T	A	B
X	E	U	P	A	R	R	O	T
S	R	T	L	X	A	O	N	E
Y	R	O	P	N	C	P	I	W
N	E	M	T	M	C	I	S	H
E	T	U	Q	P	O	C	E	A
R	L	N	Y	B	O	A	N	T
A	I	C	T	T	N	L	N	S
Y	T	H	R	R	A	F	A	E
T	A	Y	A	O	K	I	U	W
U	G	E	C	K	O	S	Z	L
M	N	U	A	A	F	H	N	M

boa	ferret	tarantula
raccoon	gecko	tortoise
parrot	tropical fish	Munchy

VERSE ON THE WING

Color and cut out the birds and hang them by a string in your bedroom window or above your bed. Then memorize the verses to help you remember how special you are to God.

Aren't two sparrows sold
for only a penny?
But your Father knows when any
one of them falls to the ground.
Even the hairs on your head are counted.
So don't be afraid!
You are worth much more
than many sparrows.
Matthew 10:29-31, CEV

Look at the birds in the sky!
They don't plant or harvest.
They don't even store grain in barns.
Yet your Father in heaven takes care of them.
Aren't you worth more than birds?
Matthew 6:26, CEV

82

MARCO'S SURVIVAL FOOD

MARCO'S GORP

1 cup peanuts

1 cup M&M's

1 cup dried banana chips

1 cup sunflower seeds

1 cup raisins

Mix all together and store in Ziploc bags.

HOT CHOCOLATE MIX

1 box powdered milk (one that will make five to six quarts)

$1/2$ cup powdered sugar

1 cup Nestlé Quick

$1/2$ cup Cremora non-dairy creamer

1 box instant chocolate pudding

$1/4$ cup powdered cocoa

Mix up all these dry ingredients and store in a dry, covered container or jar. Put $1/3$ cup mix in one cup hot water, stir, and serve! Good on a winter afternoon.

JAKE & MARCO'S BACKPACK GAME

This is a great game for groups or parties. Pick ten different items to put in a backpack. These can be just about anything that will fit: flashlight, curlers, cards, and so on. One at a time, put each item out on a table for everyone to see. Leave them out for one minute, then put all of the items back in the backpack.

Next, hand out a piece of paper and a pencil to each person. The one who can remember and write down all ten items wins! (You can make this harder by increasing the number of items. You can also do it in teams. Team 1 fills the backpack and lets Team 2 try to list the items. Then trade and let Team 2 fill the backpack, while Team 1 guesses. The team with the most correct guesses wins!)

FUN WOLF QUESTIONS & ANSWERS

1. WHAT KIND OF FAMILIES DO WOLVES HAVE?

Wolves live in family groups called packs. A pack is usually made up of a male parent, a female parent, their pups, and a few other adult wolves, who are usually the older brothers and sisters. Pack members hunt for food and help take care of the pups.

2. WHAT DO WOLVES EAT?

Wolves are predators. That means they kill and eat other animals for food. Depending on where they live, wolves feed mainly on the meat animals that have hooves, such as deer, moose, elk, or bison. They also eat beavers, rabbits, and small rodents, such as mice. Wolves do not eat humans. In fact, wolves are usually very shy around people and try to avoid them in the wild.

3. WHERE DO WOLVES LIVE?

Wolves once lived throughout most of the United States. Now they remain only in a few places. Alaska has five thousand to six thousand wolves. In most states, wolves are on the Endangered Species List, which means that our government is working to protect them because they are in danger of becoming extinct.

4. HOW HAVE WOLVES BECOME ENDANGERED?

For a long time, most people thought wolves were dangerous to humans. People were paid by the government to kill wolves. And because wolves prey on livestock (such as cows, sheep, and pigs), many wolves were poisoned. Another reason has to do with the growing human population. People and wolves both need land in order to live and raise their families. As our population has grown, the amount of wilderness where wolves can live (their habitat) has become smaller. Protecting the wolves' habitat helps protect the wolves.

5. HOW DO BABY WOLVES GROW?

Baby wolves are called pups or cubs. Usually, four to six pups are born together. The little group is called a litter, and the pups in a litter are called litter mates. They usually live in a den, which can be a small cave or a hole dug in the ground. Pups grow quickly. About twelve to fifteen days after they are born, they open their eyes for the first time. At first, they live only on milk from their mother. They start eating meat when they are three weeks old. First, adult wolves chew and swallow the meat. Then the pups lick the adult's mouth, and the food comes back up so the pups can eat it too! This sounds terrible, but wolf pups love it! When pups are six months old, they look almost like adult wolves and start hunting with the rest of the pack.

6. WHAT DO WOLF PUPS DO ALL DAY?

Wolf pups love to play. They chase each other and roll around the way dog puppies do. Many of their games appear to be a sort of practice for the things they will do as adult wolves. Pups have been observed playing with "toys" (like bones, feathers, or the skins of dead animals). They "kill" the toys over and over again and carry them around as trophies. As they get larger, they begin to hunt small animals, like rabbits. Soon they will join the pack for their first real hunt for large animals.

Thank you to the wonderful Web site at www.wolf.org for all this interesting information! Also, to read about and see pictures of a real ranch in New Mexico where hybrid wolf-dogs are kept until they are adopted, visit www.inetdesign.com/candykitchen/.

YELLOW EYES IN THE DARK

Made in the USA
Middletown, DE
27 November 2015